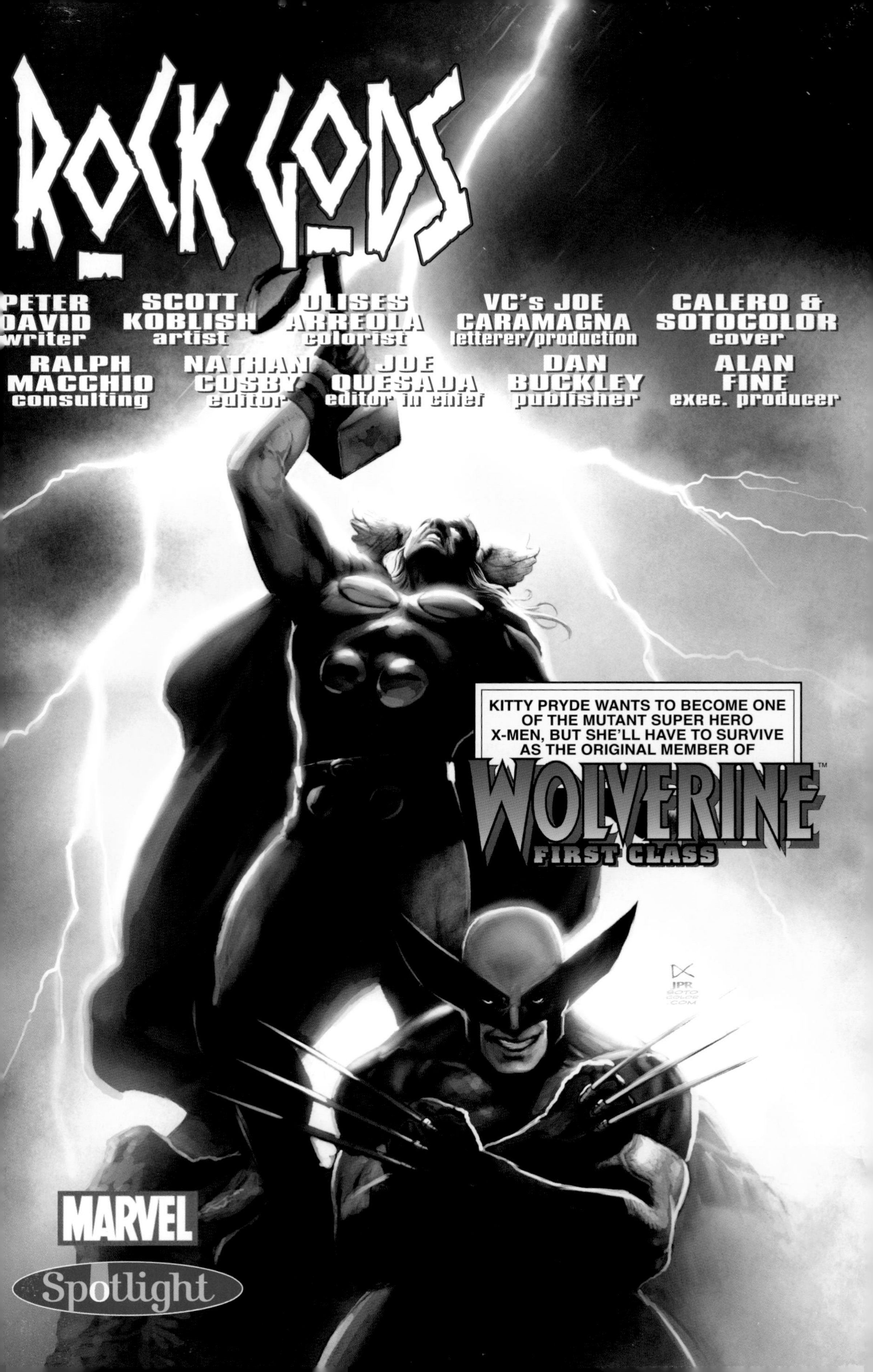
ROCK GODS
PETER DAVID writer
SCOTT KOBLISH artist
ULISES ARREOLA colorist
VC's JOE CARAMAGNA letterer/production
CALERO & SOTOCOLOR cover
RALPH MACCHIO consulting
NATHAN COSBY editor
JOE QUESADA editor in chief
DAN BUCKLEY publisher
ALAN FINE exec. producer
KITTY PRYDE WANTS TO BECOME ONE OF THE MUTANT SUPER HERO X-MEN, BUT SHE'LL HAVE TO SURVIVE AS THE ORIGINAL MEMBER OF
WOLVERINE™ FIRST CLASS
JPR SOTO COLOR COM
MARVEL
Spotlight

Visit us at www.abdopublishing.com

Reinforced library bound editions published in 2014 by Spotlight, a division of the ABDO Group, PO Box 398166, Minneapolis, MN 55439. Spotlight produces high-quality reinforced library bound editions for schools and libraries. Published by agreement with Marvel Characters, Inc.

Printed in the United States of America, North Mankato, Minnesota.
042013
092013
♻ This book contains at least 10% recycled material.

marvel.com
© 2013 Marvel

Library of Congress Cataloging-in-Publication Data

David, Peter (Peter Allen)
 Rock gods / story by Peter David ; art by Scott Koblish. -- Reinforced library bound edition.
     pages cm. -- (Wolverine, first class)
 "Marvel."
 Summary: "Kitty Pryde's got a crush, and she's depending on Wolvie to help her get the hook-up. But what can she really expect him to do when that crush is Thor?"-- Provided by publisher.
 ISBN 978-1-61479-180-5
 1. Graphic novels. [1. Graphic novels. 2. Superheroes--Fiction.] I. Koblish, Scott, illustrator. II. Title.
 PZ7.7.D374Ro 2013
 741.5'352--dc23
                            2013005935

All Spotlight books are reinforced library bindings
and manufactured in the United States of America.

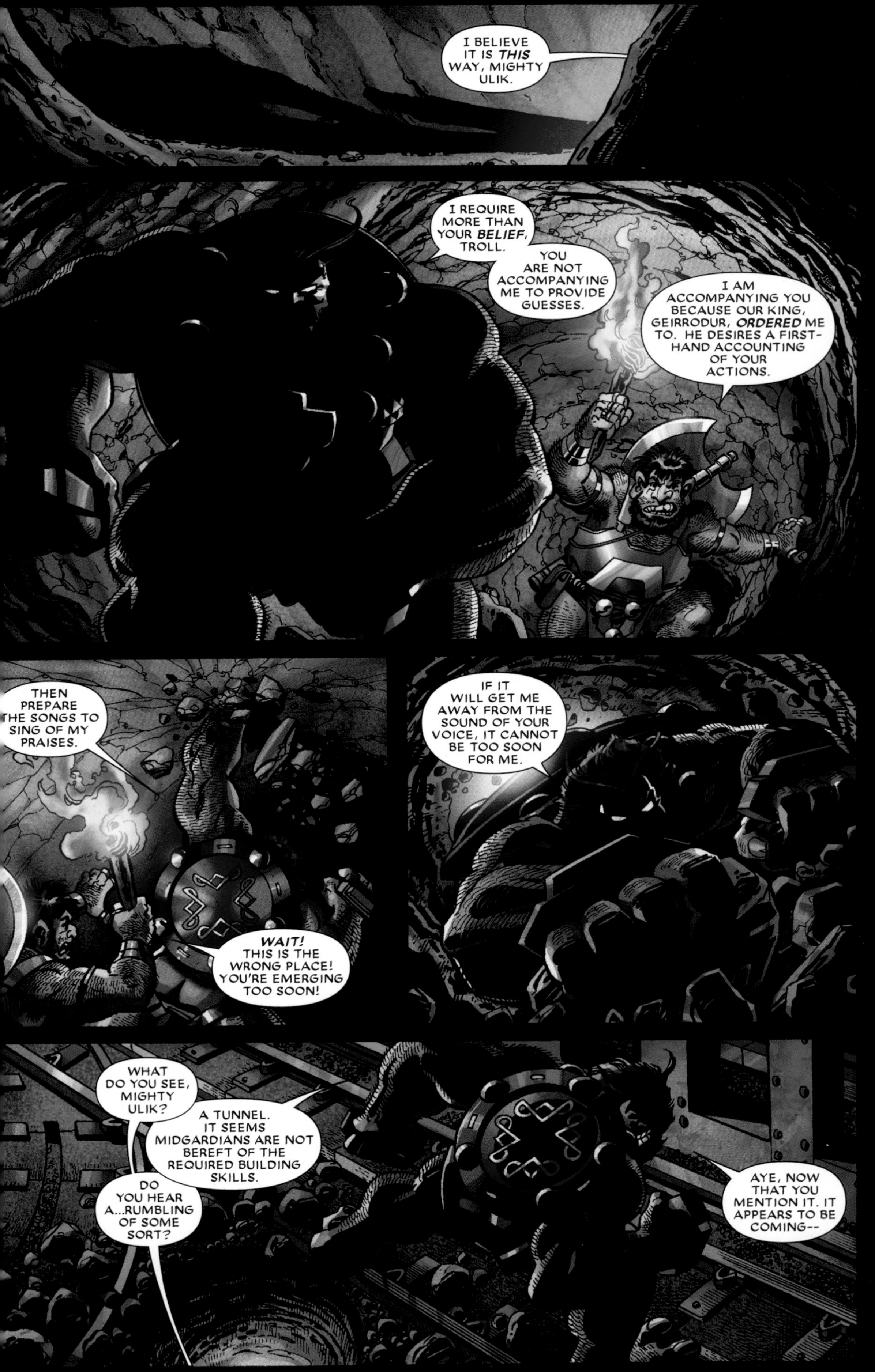
I BELIEVE IT IS THIS WAY, MIGHTY ULIK.
I REQUIRE MORE THAN YOUR BELIEF, TROLL.
YOU ARE NOT ACCOMPANYING ME TO PROVIDE GUESSES.
I AM ACCOMPANYING YOU BECAUSE OUR KING, GEIRRODUR, ORDERED ME TO. HE DESIRES A FIRST-HAND ACCOUNTING OF YOUR ACTIONS.
THEN PREPARE THE SONGS TO SING OF MY PRAISES.
WAIT! THIS IS THE WRONG PLACE! YOU'RE EMERGING TOO SOON!
IF IT WILL GET ME AWAY FROM THE SOUND OF YOUR VOICE, IT CANNOT BE TOO SOON FOR ME.
WHAT DO YOU SEE, MIGHTY ULIK?
A TUNNEL. IT SEEMS MIDGARDIANS ARE NOT BEREFT OF THE REQUIRED BUILDING SKILLS.
DO YOU HEAR A...RUMBLING OF SOME SORT?
AYE, NOW THAT YOU MENTION IT. IT APPEARS TO BE COMING--

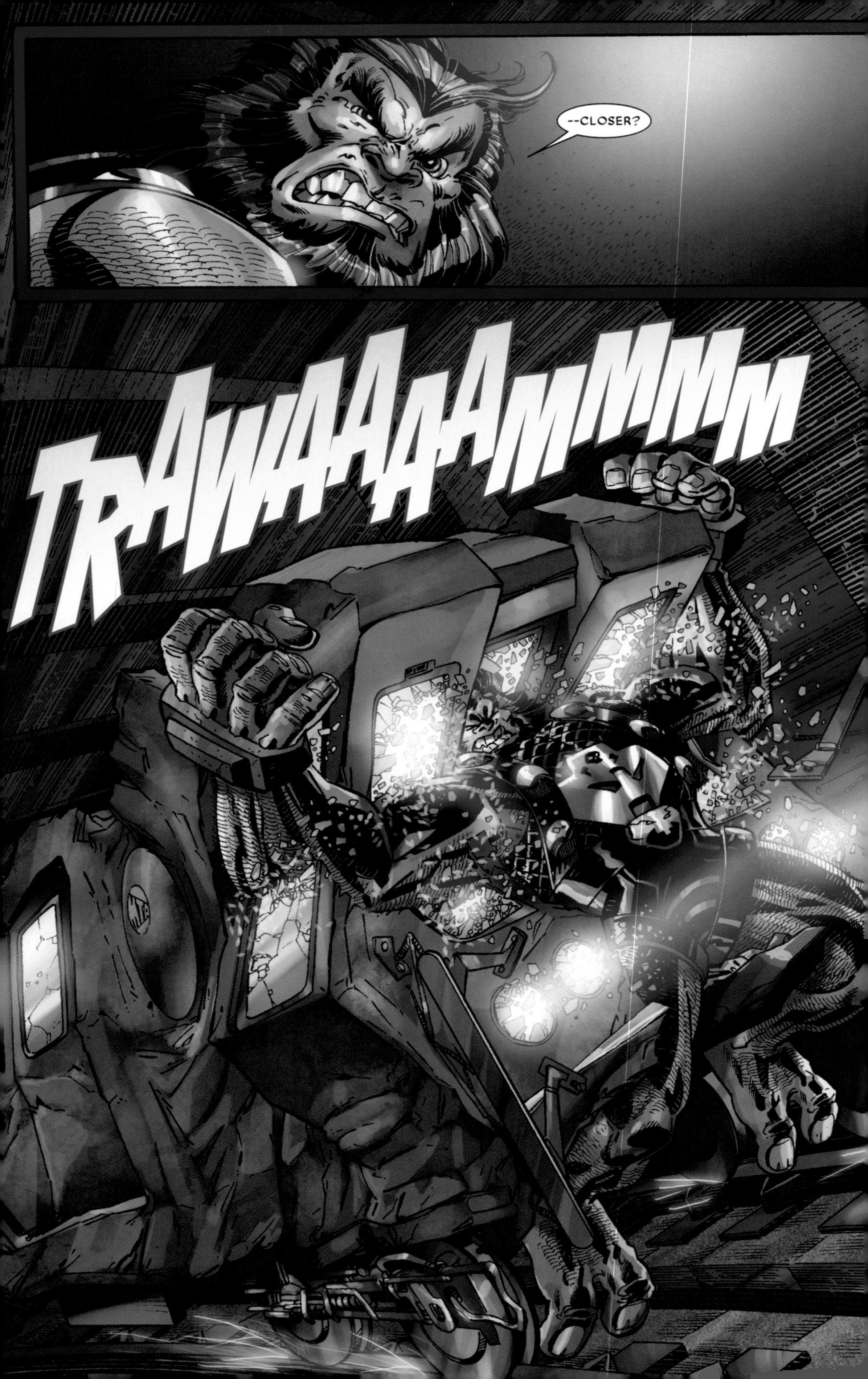
--CLOSER?
TRAWAAAAAMMMMM

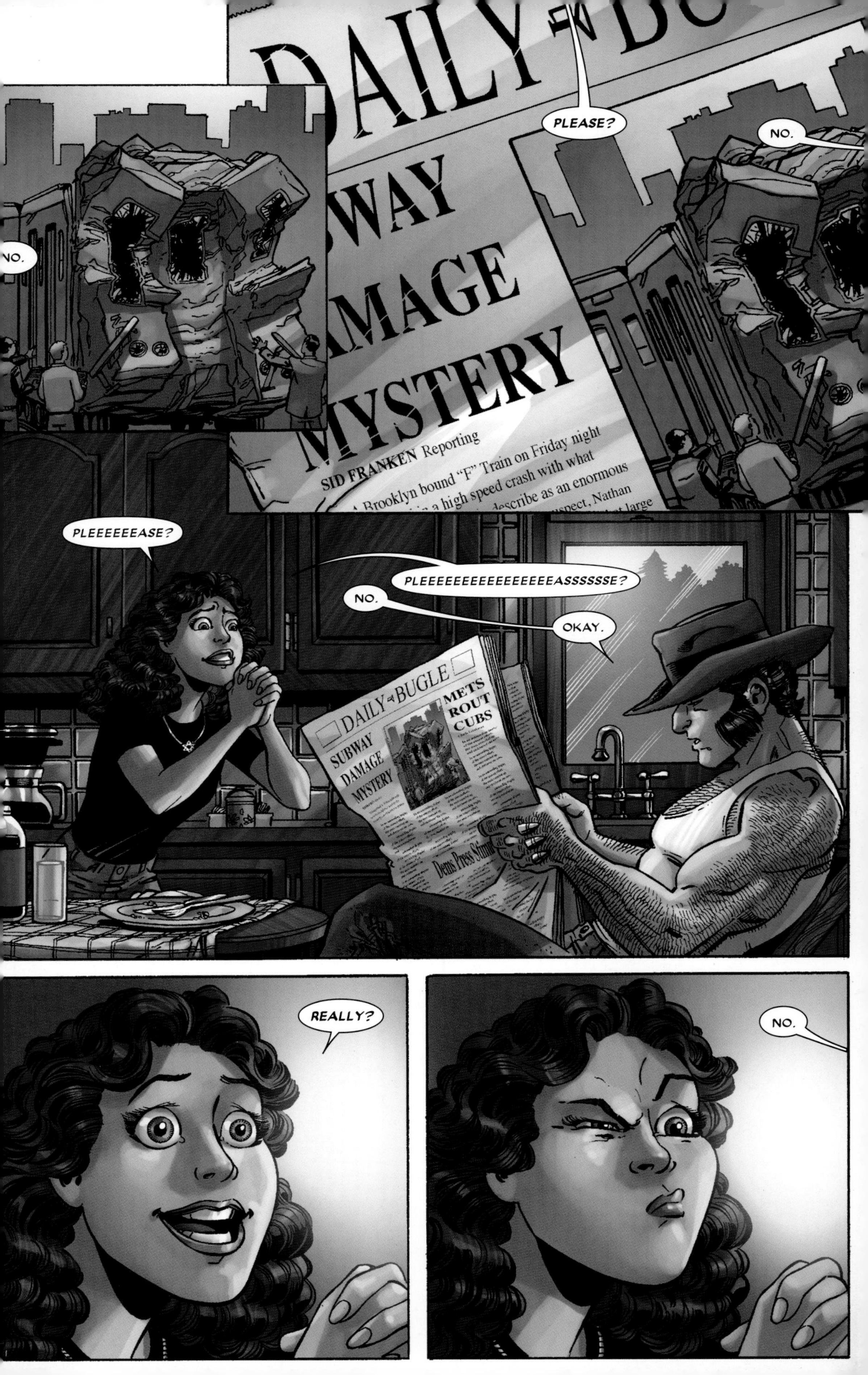

DAILY BU
SUBWAY DAMAGE MYSTERY
SID FRANKEN Reporting
A Brooklyn bound "F" Train on Friday night
a high speed crash with what
describe as an enormous
spect, Nathan
NO.
PLEASE?
NO.
PLEEEEEEEASE?
PLEEEEEEEEEEEEEEEEEEASSSSSSE?
NO.
OKAY.
DAILY BUGLE
SUBWAY DAMAGE MYSTERY
METS ROUT CUBS
REALLY?
NO.

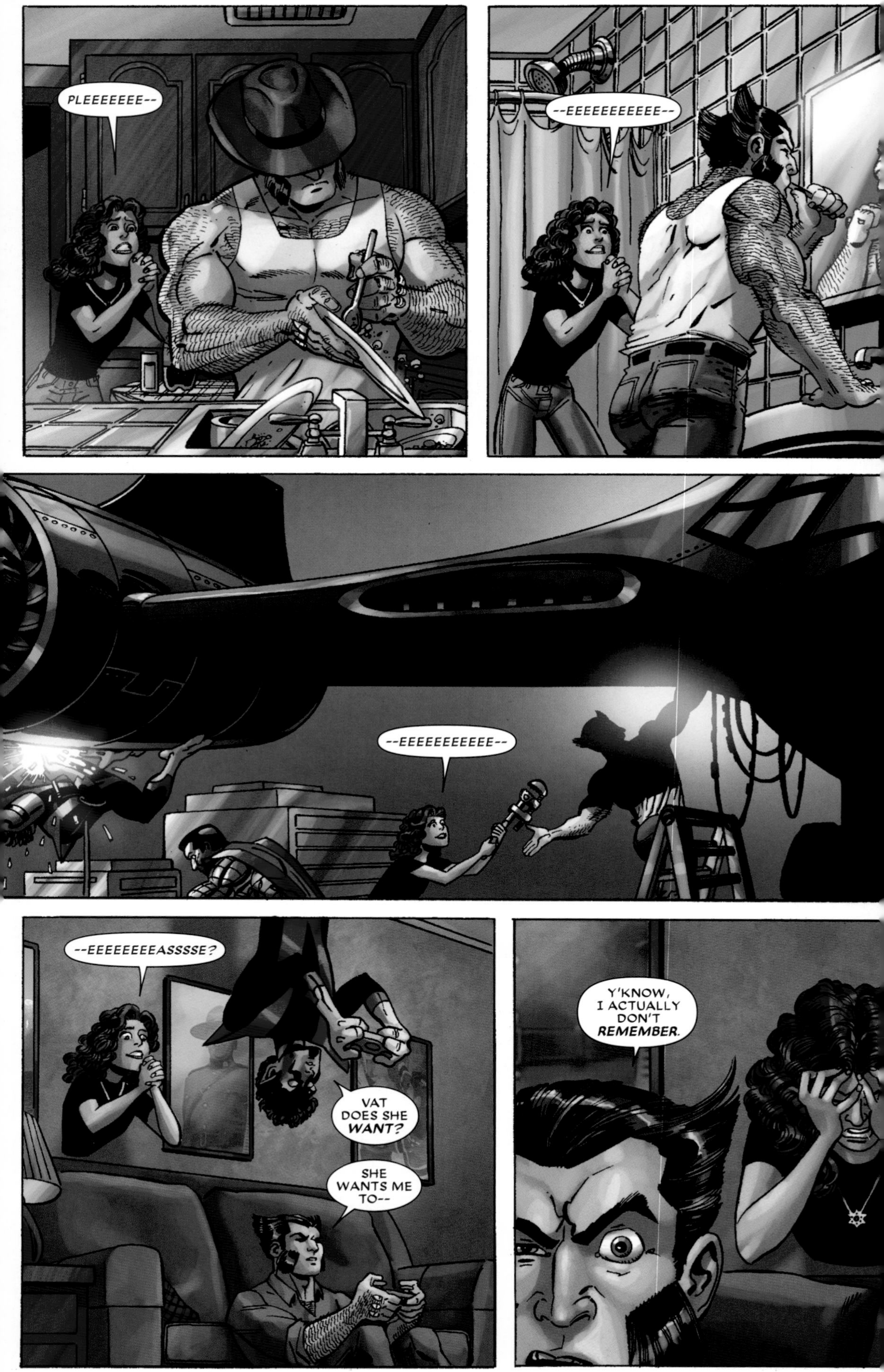
PLEEEEEEE--
--EEEEEEEEEEE--
--EEEEEEEEEEE--
--EEEEEEEASSSSE?
VAT DOES SHE *WANT?*
SHE WANTS ME TO--
Y'KNOW, I ACTUALLY DON'T *REMEMBER.*

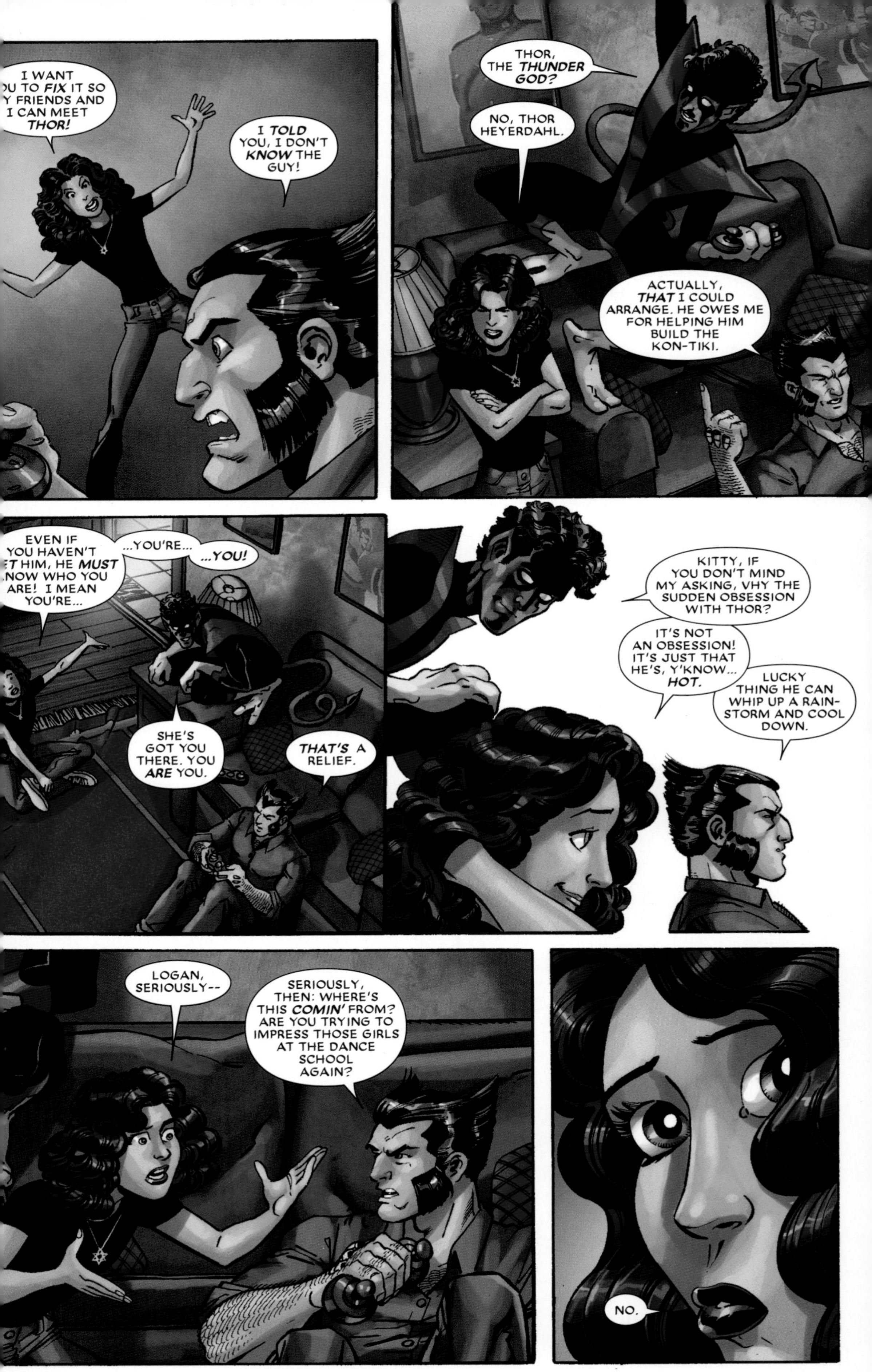
I WANT
U TO FIX IT SO
Y FRIENDS AND
I CAN MEET
THOR!
I TOLD YOU, I DON'T KNOW THE GUY!
THOR, THE THUNDER GOD?
NO, THOR HEYERDAHL.
ACTUALLY, THAT I COULD ARRANGE. HE OWES ME FOR HELPING HIM BUILD THE KON-TIKI.
EVEN IF YOU HAVEN'T
T HIM, HE MUST
NOW WHO YOU
ARE! I MEAN YOU'RE...
...YOU'RE...
...YOU!
SHE'S GOT YOU THERE. YOU ARE YOU.
THAT'S A RELIEF.
KITTY, IF YOU DON'T MIND MY ASKING, VHY THE SUDDEN OBSESSION WITH THOR?
IT'S NOT AN OBSESSION! IT'S JUST THAT HE'S, Y'KNOW... HOT.
LUCKY THING HE CAN WHIP UP A RAIN-STORM AND COOL DOWN.
LOGAN, SERIOUSLY--
SERIOUSLY, THEN: WHERE'S THIS COMIN' FROM? ARE YOU TRYING TO IMPRESS THOSE GIRLS AT THE DANCE SCHOOL AGAIN?
NO.

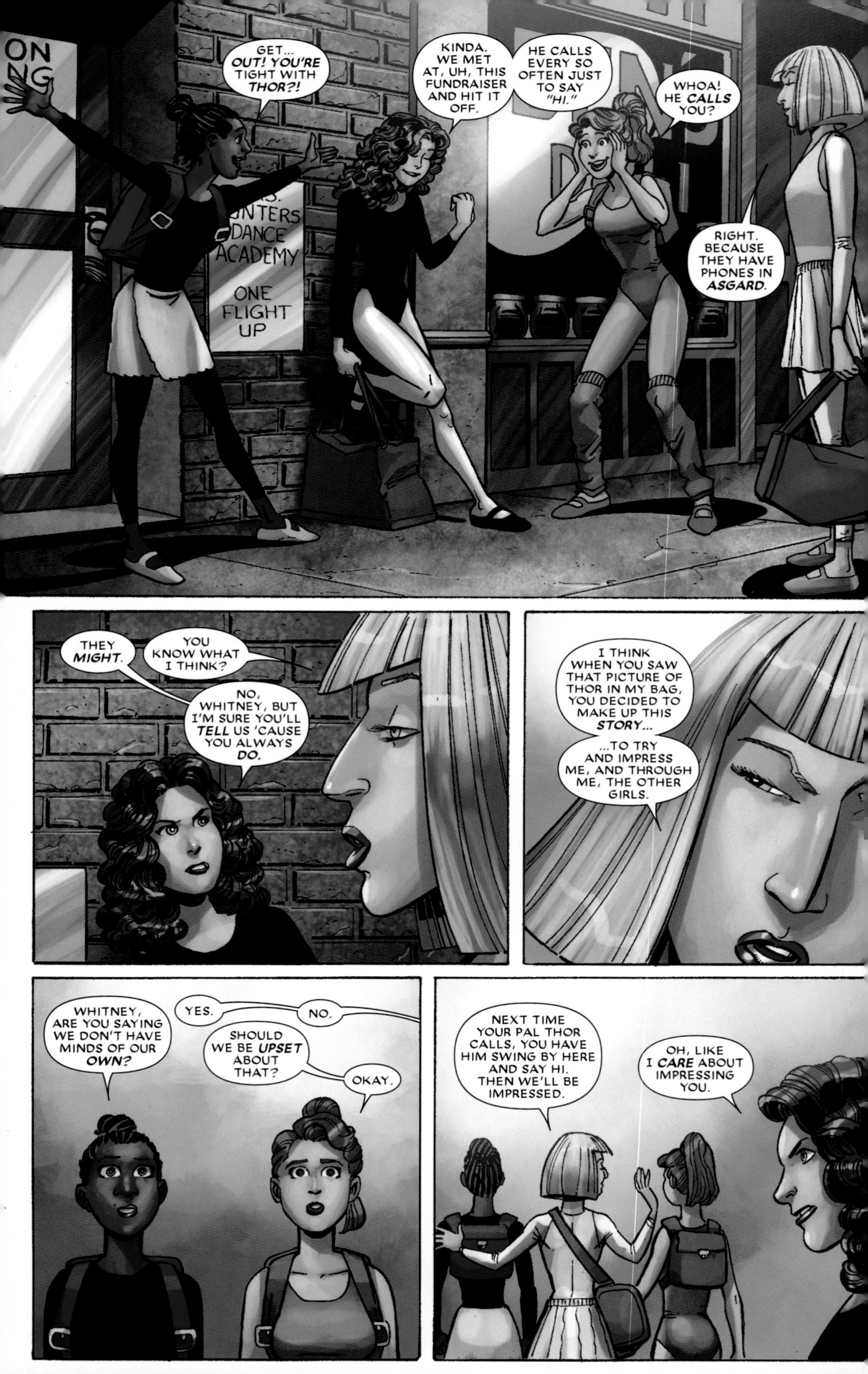
ON
NG
S. UNTERS DANCE ACADEMY
ONE FLIGHT UP
GET... OUT! YOU'RE TIGHT WITH THOR?!
KINDA. WE MET AT, UH, THIS FUNDRAISER AND HIT IT OFF.
HE CALLS EVERY SO OFTEN JUST TO SAY "HI."
WHOA! HE CALLS YOU?
RIGHT. BECAUSE THEY HAVE PHONES IN ASGARD.
THEY MIGHT.
YOU KNOW WHAT I THINK?
NO, WHITNEY, BUT I'M SURE YOU'LL TELL US 'CAUSE YOU ALWAYS DO.
I THINK WHEN YOU SAW THAT PICTURE OF THOR IN MY BAG, YOU DECIDED TO MAKE UP THIS STORY...
...TO TRY AND IMPRESS ME, AND THROUGH ME, THE OTHER GIRLS.
WHITNEY, ARE YOU SAYING WE DON'T HAVE MINDS OF OUR OWN?
YES.
NO.
SHOULD WE BE UPSET ABOUT THAT?
OKAY.
NEXT TIME YOUR PAL THOR CALLS, YOU HAVE HIM SWING BY HERE AND SAY HI. THEN WE'LL BE IMPRESSED.
OH, LIKE I CARE ABOUT IMPRESSING YOU.

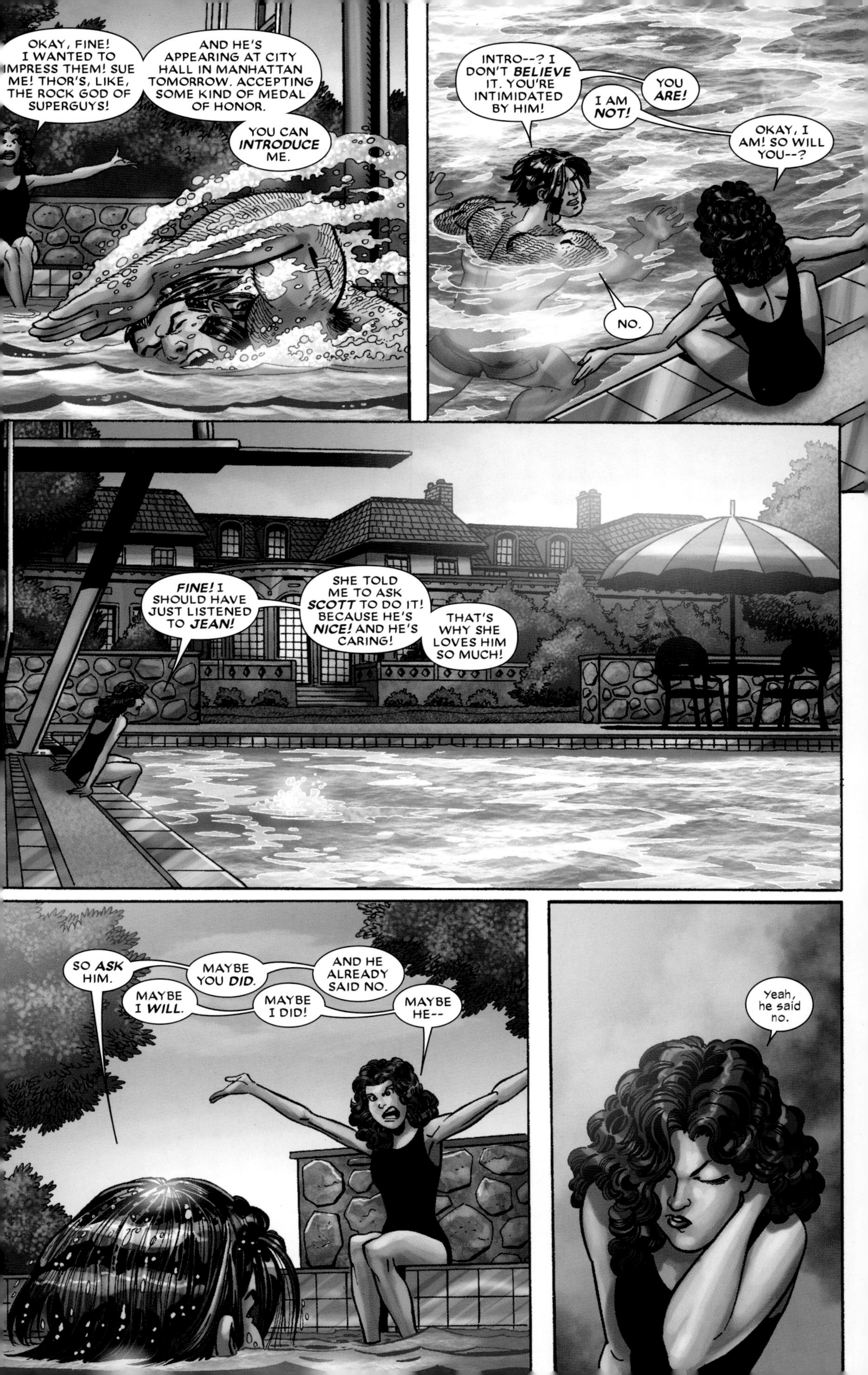
OKAY, FINE! I WANTED TO IMPRESS THEM! SUE ME! THOR'S, LIKE, THE ROCK GOD OF SUPERGUYS!
AND HE'S APPEARING AT CITY HALL IN MANHATTAN TOMORROW. ACCEPTING SOME KIND OF MEDAL OF HONOR.
YOU CAN INTRODUCE ME.
INTRO--? I DON'T BELIEVE IT. YOU'RE INTIMIDATED BY HIM!
YOU ARE!
I AM NOT!
OKAY, I AM! SO WILL YOU--?
NO.
FINE! I SHOULD HAVE JUST LISTENED TO JEAN!
SHE TOLD ME TO ASK SCOTT TO DO IT! BECAUSE HE'S NICE! AND HE'S CARING!
THAT'S WHY SHE LOVES HIM SO MUCH!
SO ASK HIM.
MAYBE I WILL.
MAYBE YOU DID.
MAYBE I DID!
AND HE ALREADY SAID NO.
MAYBE HE--
Yeah, he said no.

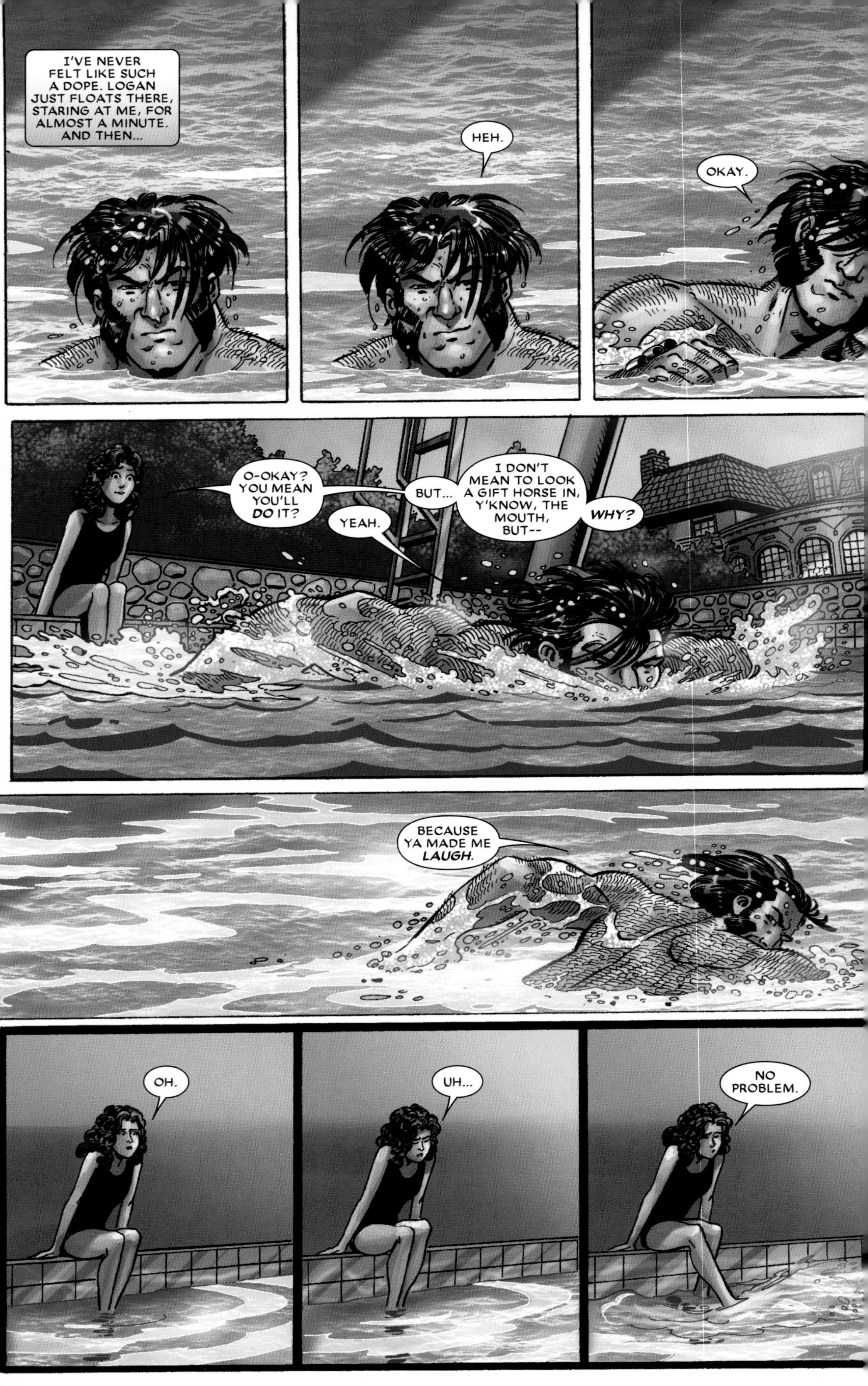
I'VE NEVER FELT LIKE SUCH A DOPE. LOGAN JUST FLOATS THERE, STARING AT ME, FOR ALMOST A MINUTE. AND THEN...
HEH.
OKAY.
O-OKAY? YOU MEAN YOU'LL DO IT?
YEAH.
BUT...
I DON'T MEAN TO LOOK A GIFT HORSE IN, Y'KNOW, THE MOUTH, BUT--
WHY?
BECAUSE YA MADE ME LAUGH.
OH.
UH...
NO PROBLEM.

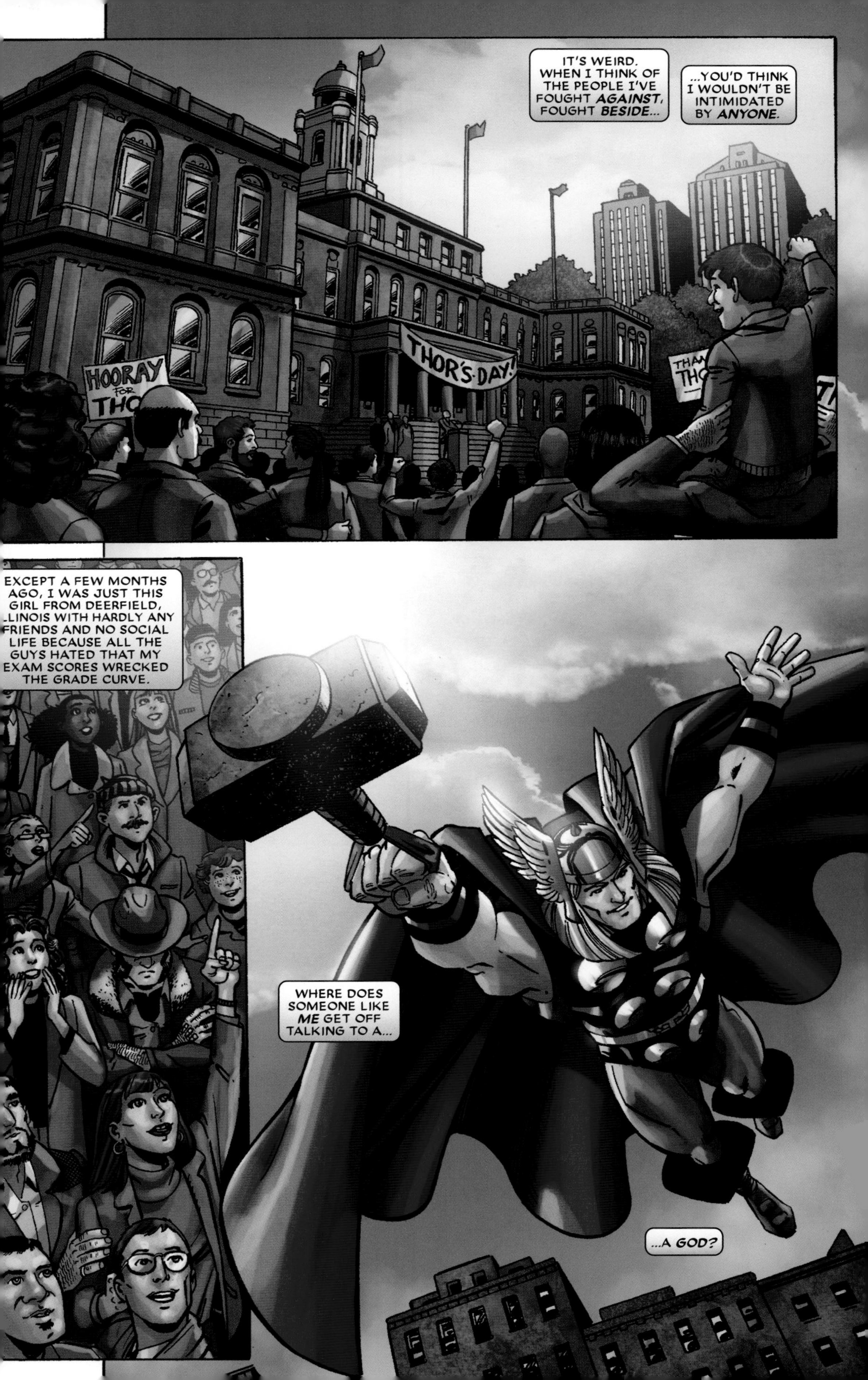
IT'S WEIRD. WHEN I THINK OF THE PEOPLE I'VE FOUGHT *AGAINST*, FOUGHT *BESIDE*...
...YOU'D THINK I WOULDN'T BE INTIMIDATED BY *ANYONE*.
HOORAY FOR THO
THOR'S-DAY!
EXCEPT A FEW MONTHS AGO, I WAS JUST THIS GIRL FROM DEERFIELD, LLINOIS WITH HARDLY ANY FRIENDS AND NO SOCIAL LIFE BECAUSE ALL THE GUYS HATED THAT MY EXAM SCORES WRECKED THE GRADE CURVE.
WHERE DOES SOMEONE LIKE *ME* GET OFF TALKING TO A...
...A *GOD*?

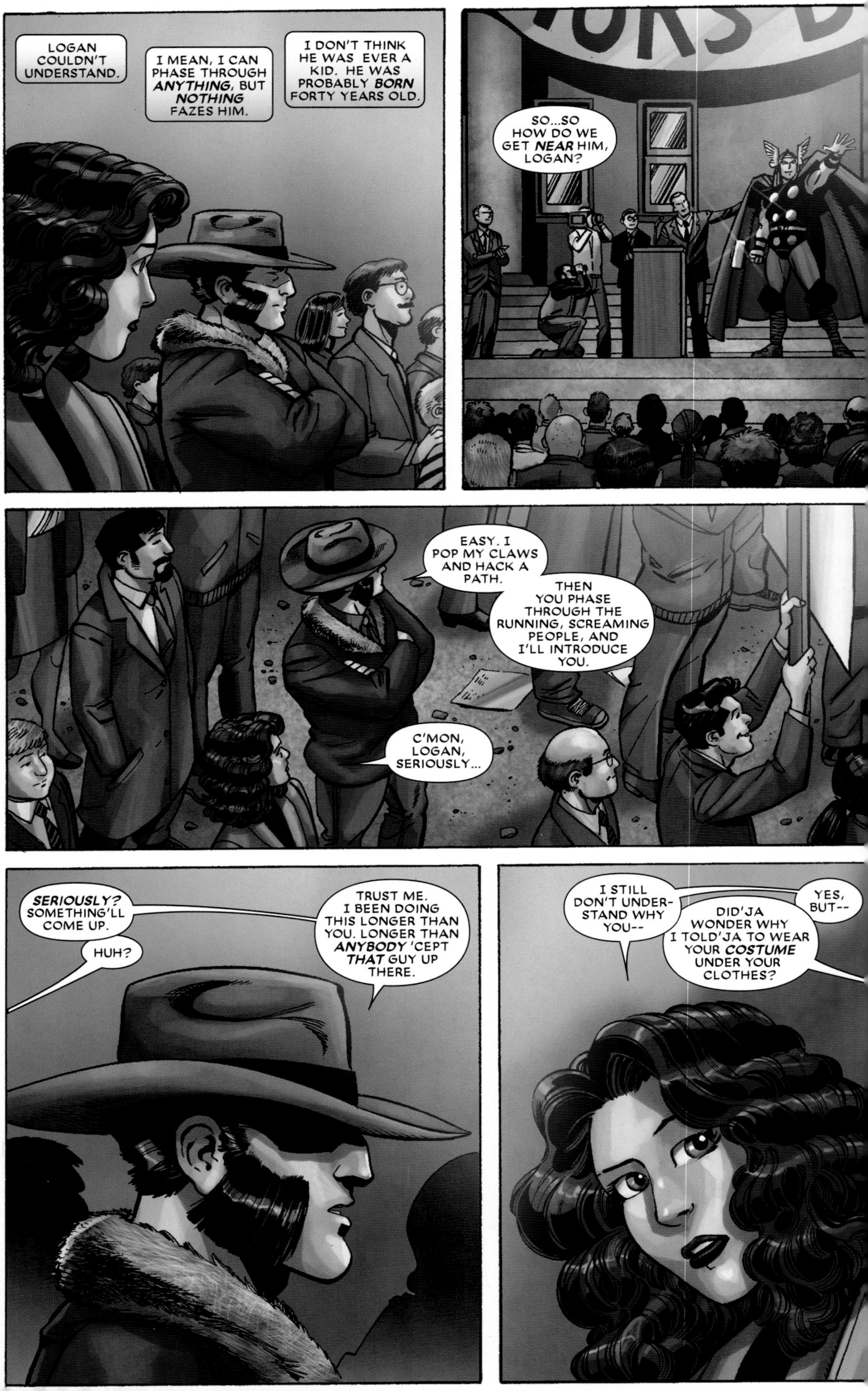
LOGAN COULDN'T UNDERSTAND.
I MEAN, I CAN PHASE THROUGH ANYTHING, BUT NOTHING FAZES HIM.
I DON'T THINK HE WAS EVER A KID. HE WAS PROBABLY BORN FORTY YEARS OLD.
SO...SO HOW DO WE GET NEAR HIM, LOGAN?
EASY. I POP MY CLAWS AND HACK A PATH.
THEN YOU PHASE THROUGH THE RUNNING, SCREAMING PEOPLE, AND I'LL INTRODUCE YOU.
C'MON, LOGAN, SERIOUSLY...
SERIOUSLY? SOMETHING'LL COME UP.
HUH?
TRUST ME. I BEEN DOING THIS LONGER THAN YOU. LONGER THAN ANYBODY 'CEPT THAT GUY UP THERE.
I STILL DON'T UNDERSTAND WHY YOU--
YES, BUT--
DID'JA WONDER WHY I TOLD'JA TO WEAR YOUR COSTUME UNDER YOUR CLOTHES?

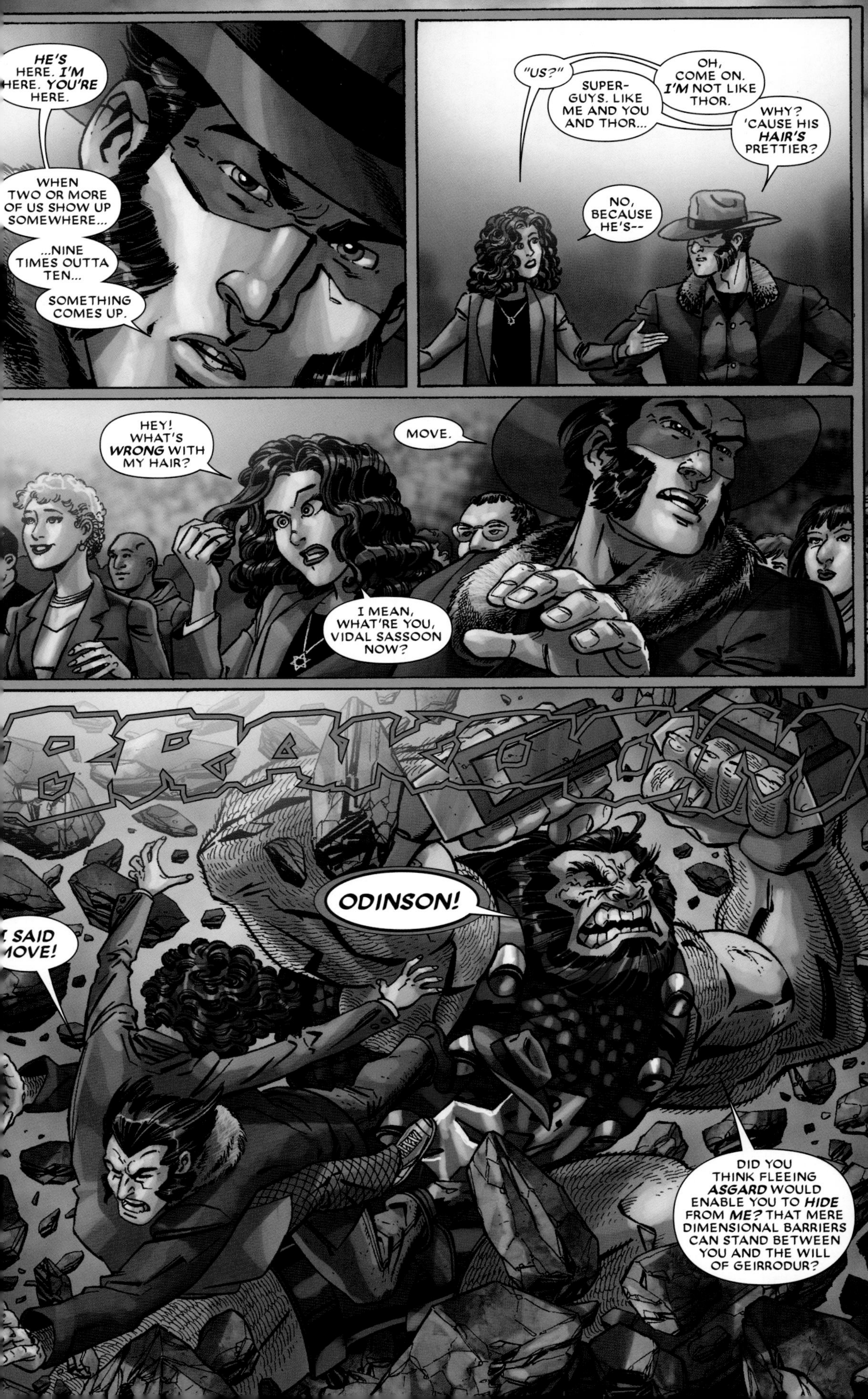
HE'S HERE. I'M HERE. YOU'RE HERE.
WHEN TWO OR MORE OF US SHOW UP SOMEWHERE...
...NINE TIMES OUTTA TEN...
SOMETHING COMES UP.
"US?"
SUPER-GUYS. LIKE ME AND YOU AND THOR...
OH, COME ON. I'M NOT LIKE THOR.
WHY? 'CAUSE HIS HAIR'S PRETTIER?
NO, BECAUSE HE'S--
HEY! WHAT'S WRONG WITH MY HAIR?
MOVE.
I MEAN, WHAT'RE YOU, VIDAL SASSOON NOW?
ODINSON!
SAID
DID YOU THINK FLEEING ASGARD WOULD ENABLE YOU TO HIDE FROM ME? THAT MERE DIMENSIONAL BARRIERS CAN STAND BETWEEN YOU AND THE WILL OF GEIRRODUR?

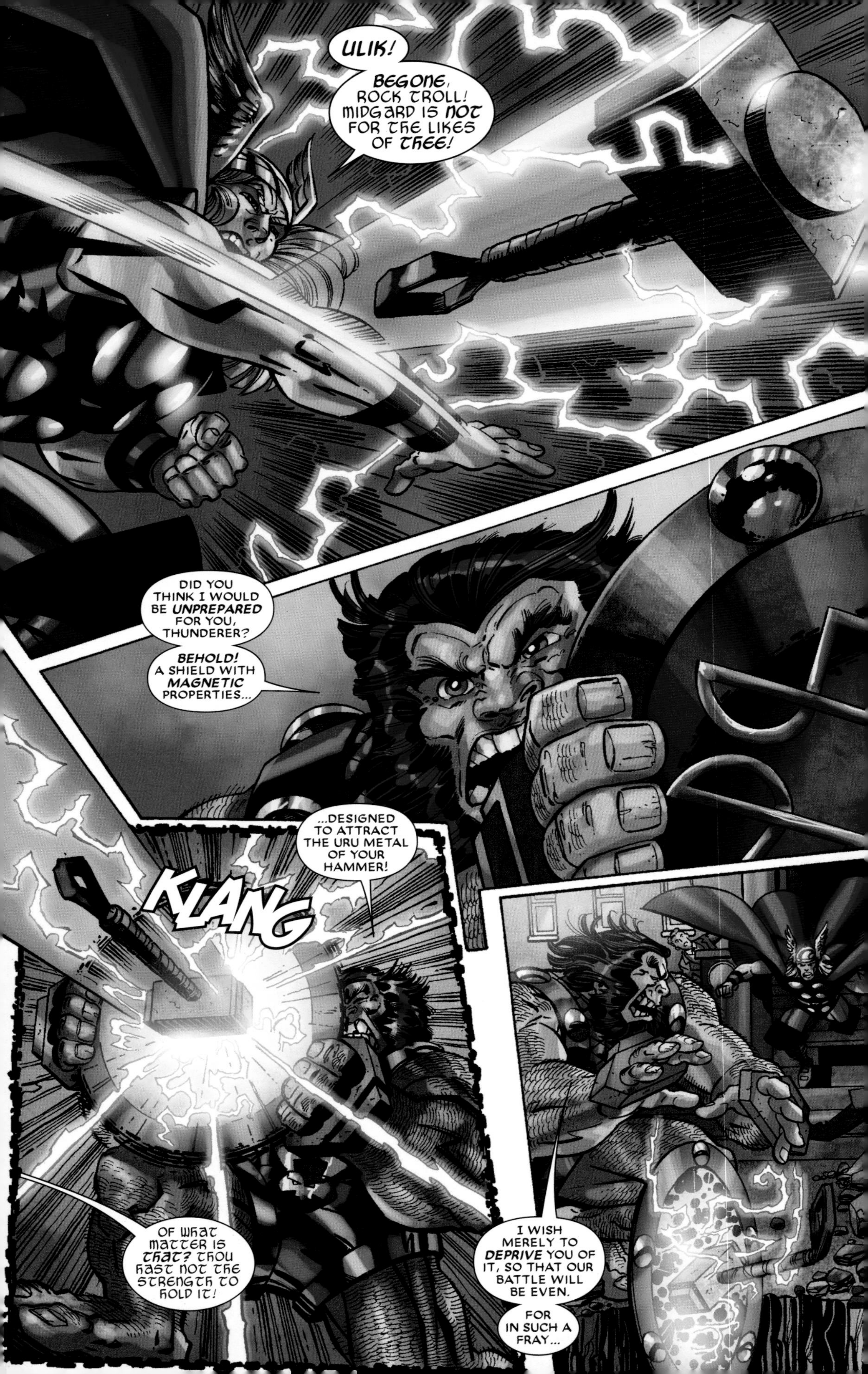
ULIK!
BEGONE, ROCK TROLL! MIDGARD IS NOT FOR THE LIKES OF THEE!
DID YOU THINK I WOULD BE UNPREPARED FOR YOU, THUNDERER?
BEHOLD! A SHIELD WITH MAGNETIC PROPERTIES...
...DESIGNED TO ATTRACT THE URU METAL OF YOUR HAMMER!
KLANG
OF WHAT MATTER IS THAT? THOU HAST NOT THE STRENGTH TO HOLD IT!
I WISH MERELY TO DEPRIVE YOU OF IT, SO THAT OUR BATTLE WILL BE EVEN.
FOR IN SUCH A FRAY...

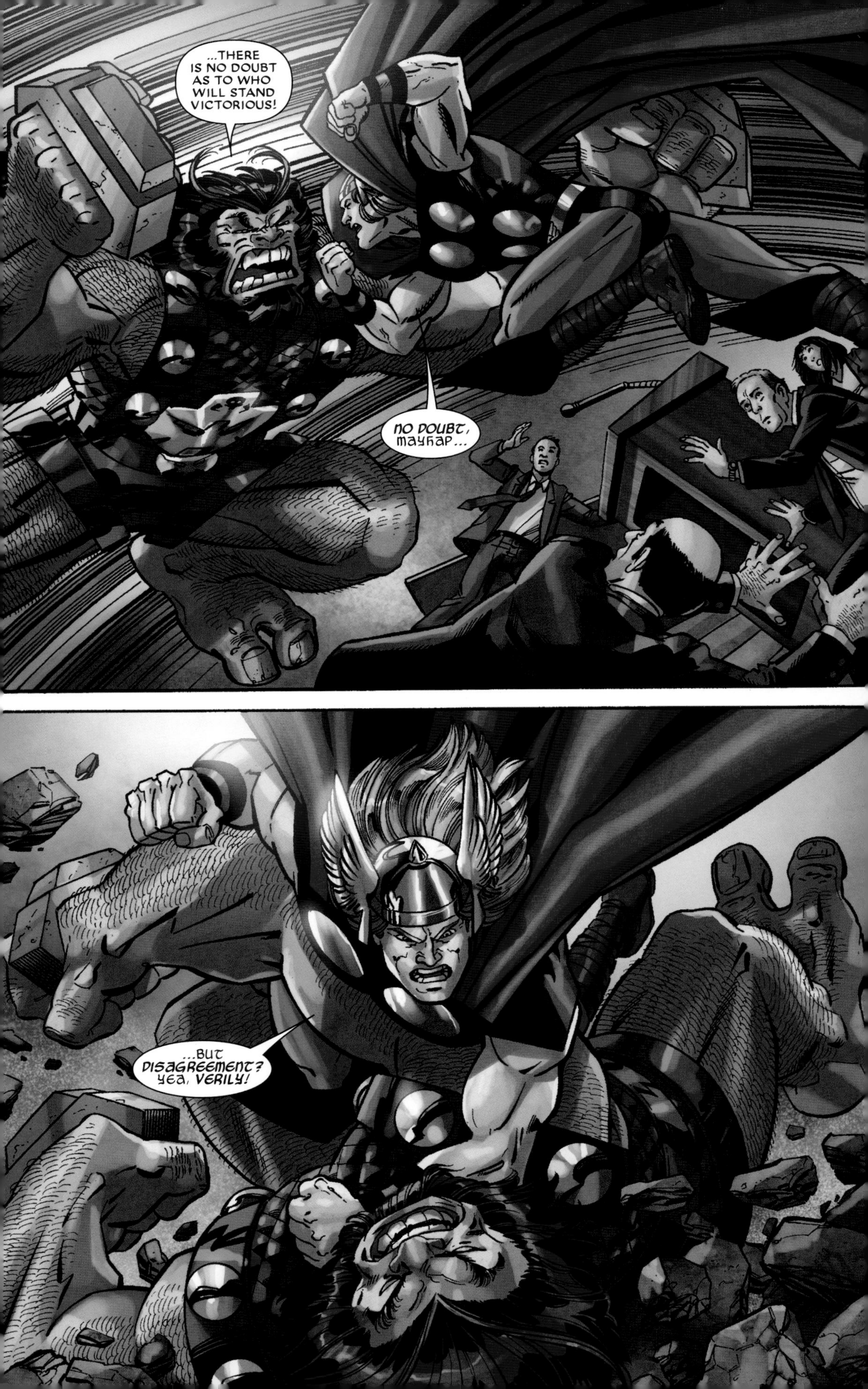
...THERE IS NO DOUBT AS TO WHO WILL STAND VICTORIOUS!
NO DOUBT, MAYHAP...
...BUT DISAGREEMENT? YEA, VERILY!

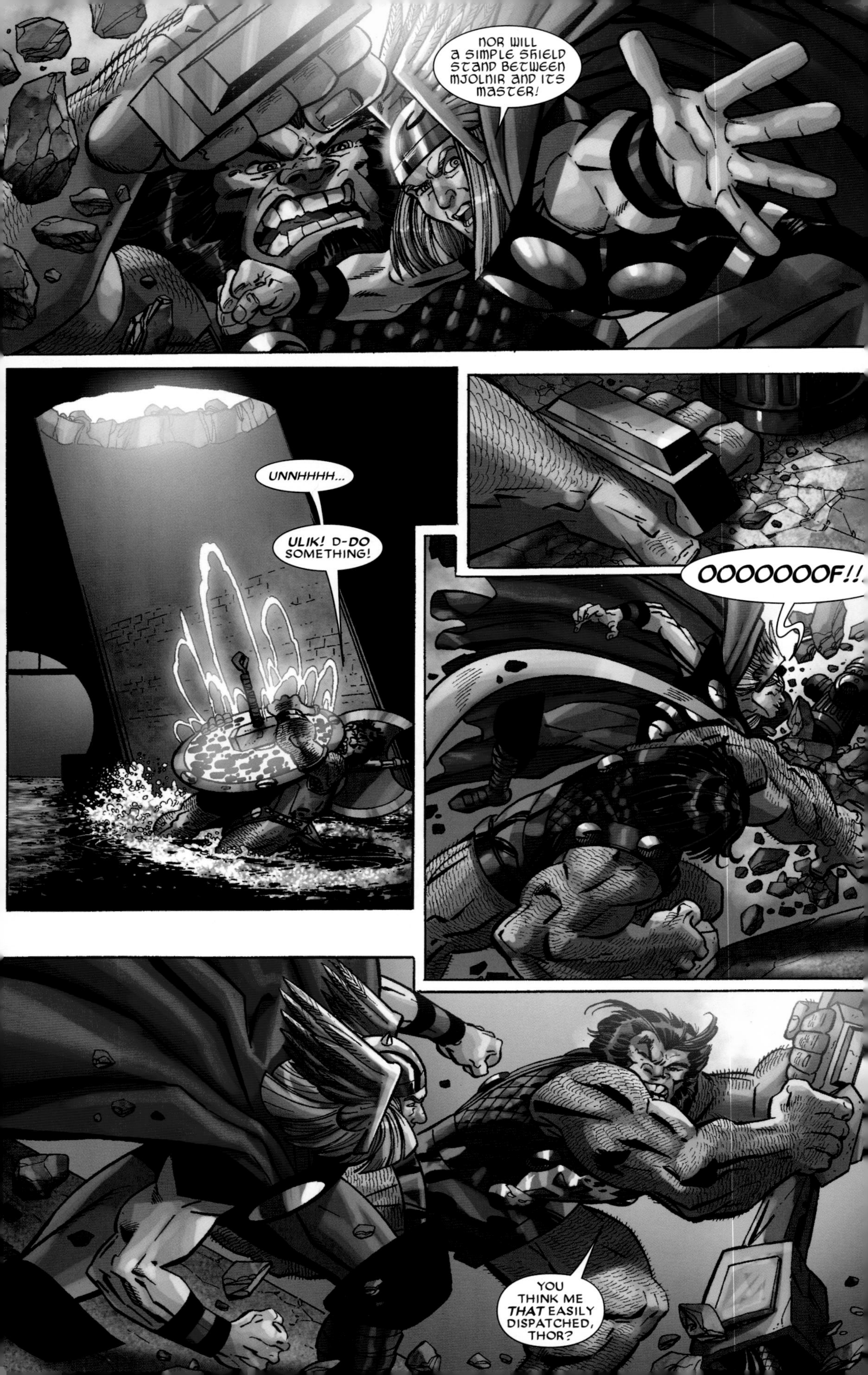
NOR WILL A SIMPLE SHIELD STAND BETWEEN MJOLNIR AND ITS MASTER!
UNNHHHH...
ULIK! D-DO SOMETHING!
OOOOOOOF!!
YOU THINK ME THAT EASILY DISPATCHED, THOR?

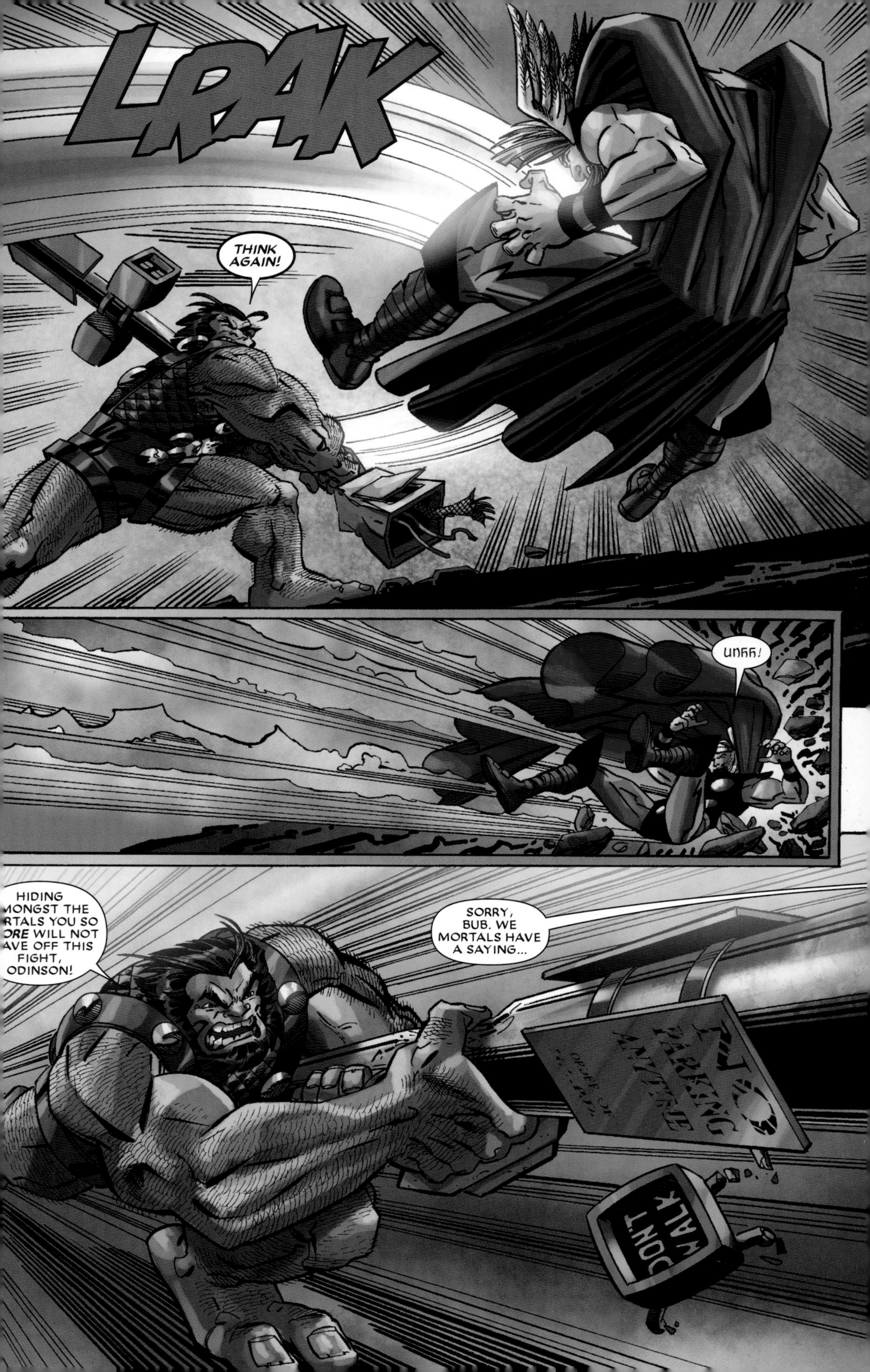
LRAK
THINK AGAIN!
UNFF!
HIDING MONGST THE RTALS YOU SO ORE WILL NOT AVE OFF THIS FIGHT, ODINSON!
SORRY, BUB. WE MORTALS HAVE A SAYING...
NO PARKING ANYTIME
DONT WALK

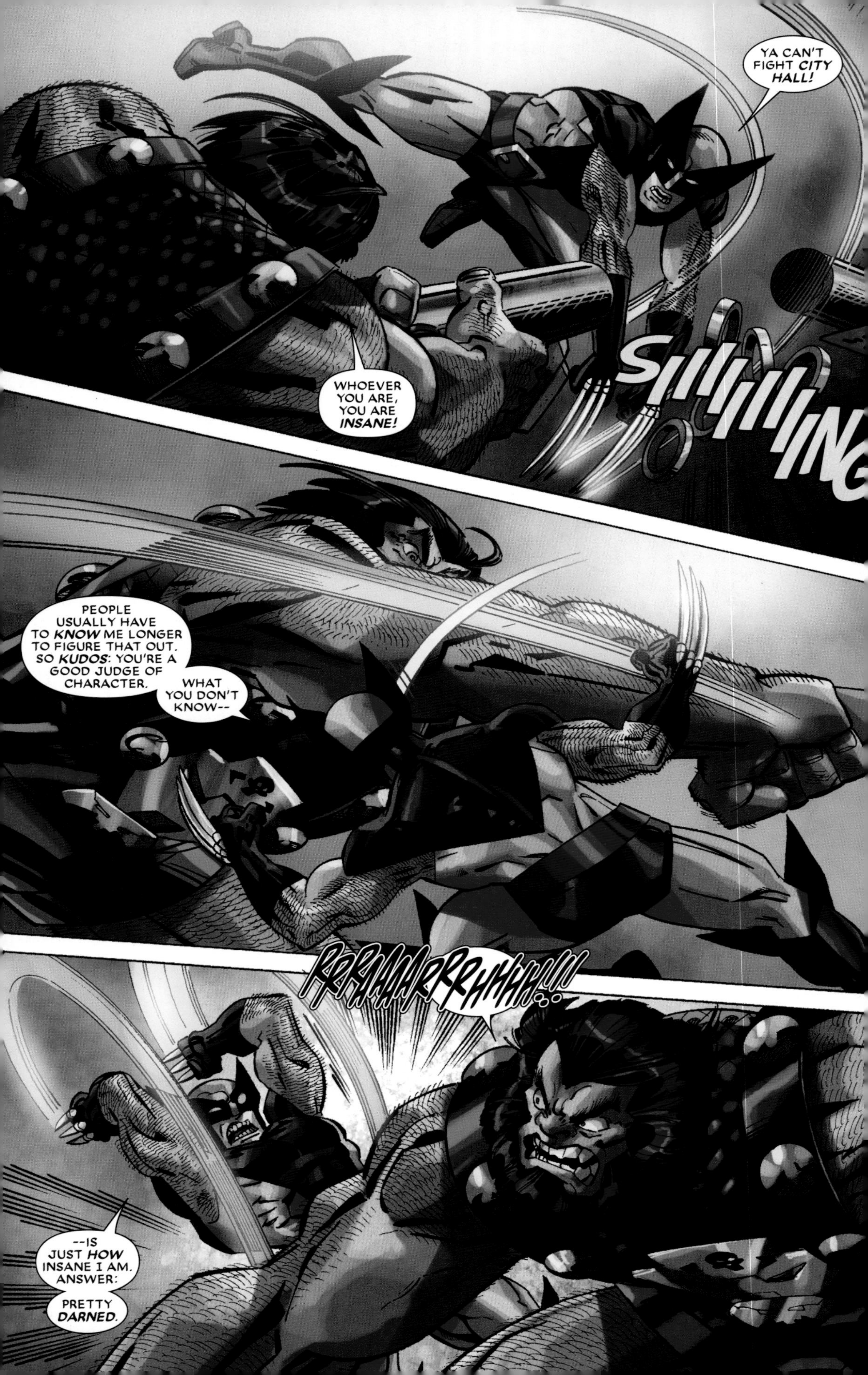
YA CAN'T FIGHT *CITY HALL!*
WHOEVER YOU ARE, YOU ARE *INSANE!*
SIIIIIIIING
PEOPLE USUALLY HAVE TO *KNOW* ME LONGER TO FIGURE THAT OUT. SO *KUDOS*: YOU'RE A GOOD JUDGE OF CHARACTER.
WHAT YOU DON'T KNOW--
RRRAAAARRRHHHH!!!
--IS JUST *HOW* INSANE I AM. ANSWER:
PRETTY *DARNED*.

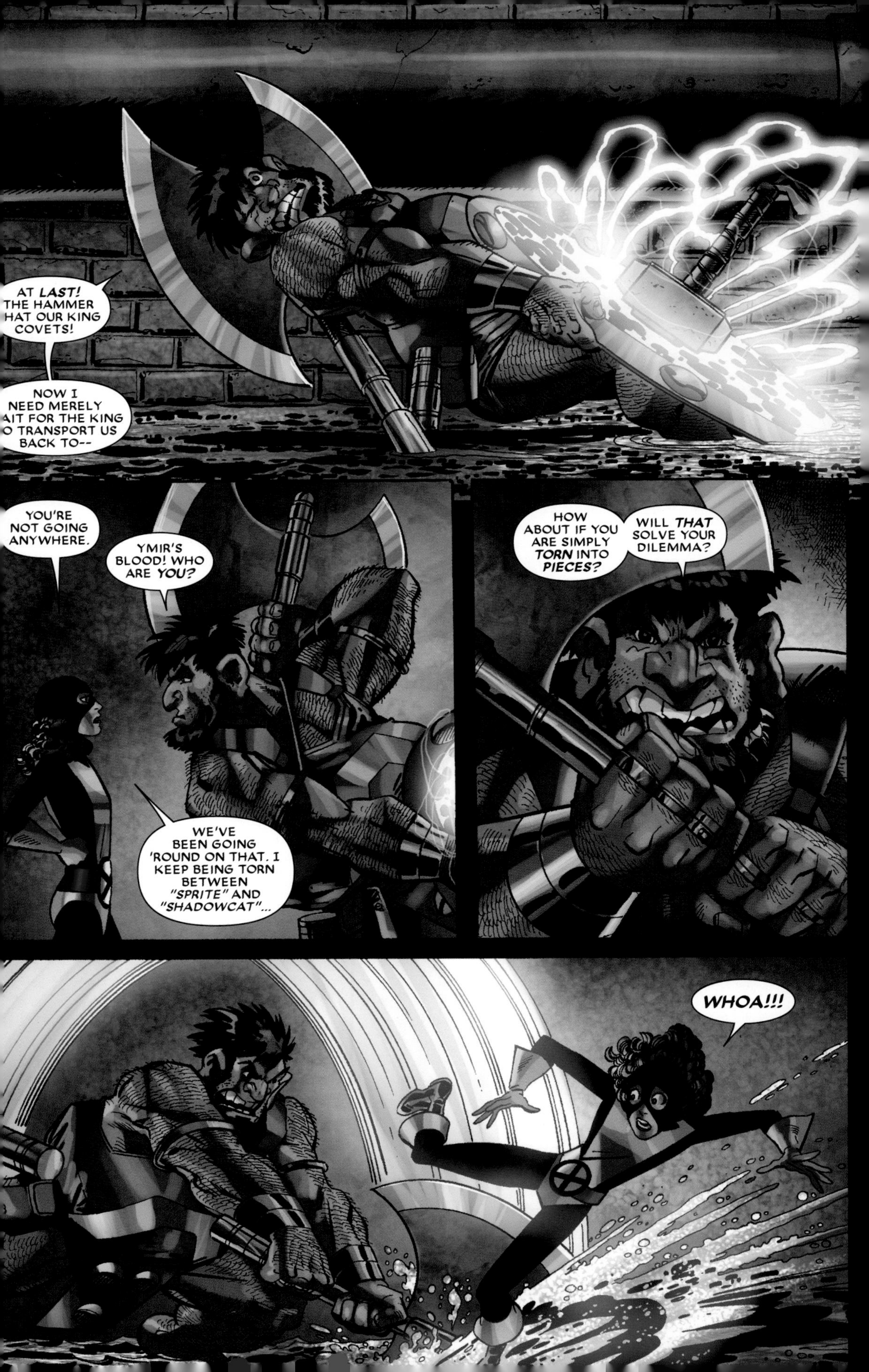
AT LAST! THE HAMMER HAT OUR KING COVETS!
NOW I NEED MERELY AIT FOR THE KING O TRANSPORT US BACK TO--
YOU'RE NOT GOING ANYWHERE.
YMIR'S BLOOD! WHO ARE YOU?
WE'VE BEEN GOING 'ROUND ON THAT. I KEEP BEING TORN BETWEEN "SPRITE" AND "SHADOWCAT"...
HOW ABOUT IF YOU ARE SIMPLY TORN INTO PIECES?
WILL THAT SOLVE YOUR DILEMMA?
WHOA!!!

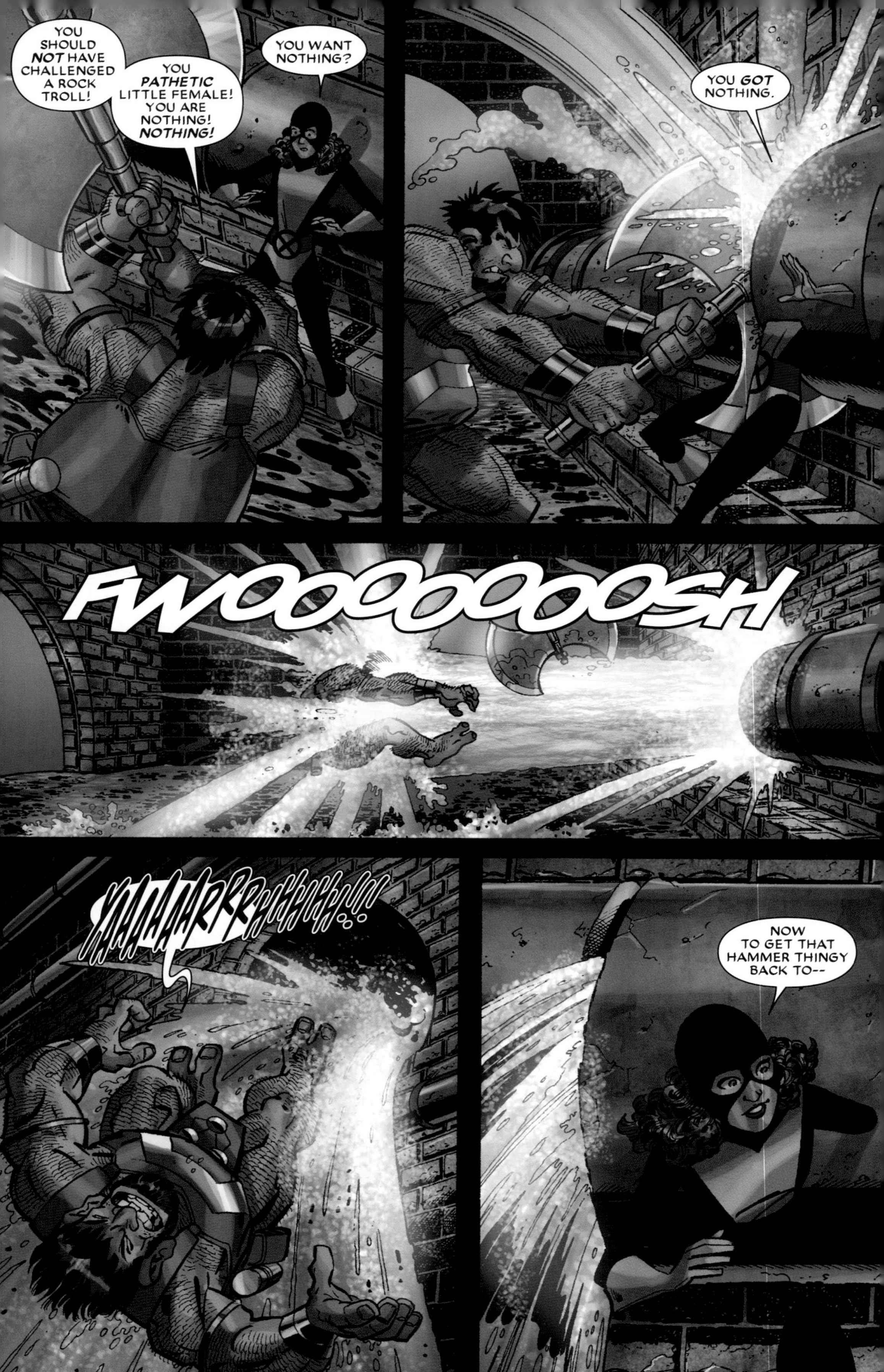
YOU SHOULD **NOT** HAVE CHALLENGED A ROCK TROLL!
YOU ***PATHETIC*** LITTLE FEMALE! YOU ARE NOTHING! ***NOTHING!***
YOU WANT NOTHING?
YOU **GOT** NOTHING.
FWOOOOOOOSH
YAAAARRRGHHHH!!!
NOW TO GET THAT HAMMER THINGY BACK TO--

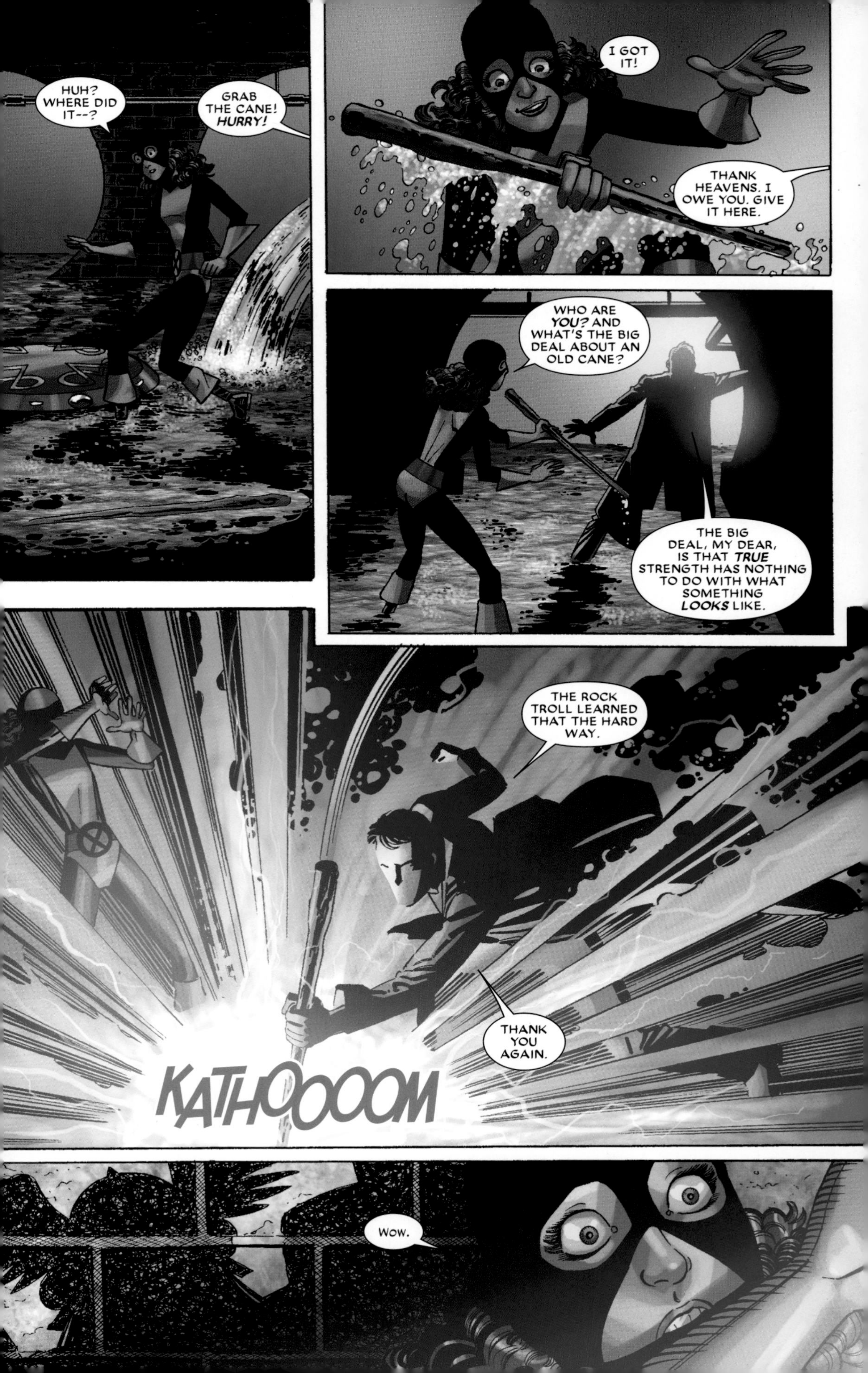
HUH? WHERE DID IT--?
GRAB THE CANE! *HURRY!*
I GOT IT!
THANK HEAVENS. I OWE YOU. GIVE IT HERE.
WHO ARE *YOU?* AND WHAT'S THE BIG DEAL ABOUT AN OLD CANE?
THE BIG DEAL, MY DEAR, IS THAT *TRUE* STRENGTH HAS NOTHING TO DO WITH WHAT SOMETHING *LOOKS* LIKE.
THE ROCK TROLL LEARNED THAT THE HARD WAY.
THANK YOU AGAIN.
KATHOOOOOM
WOW.

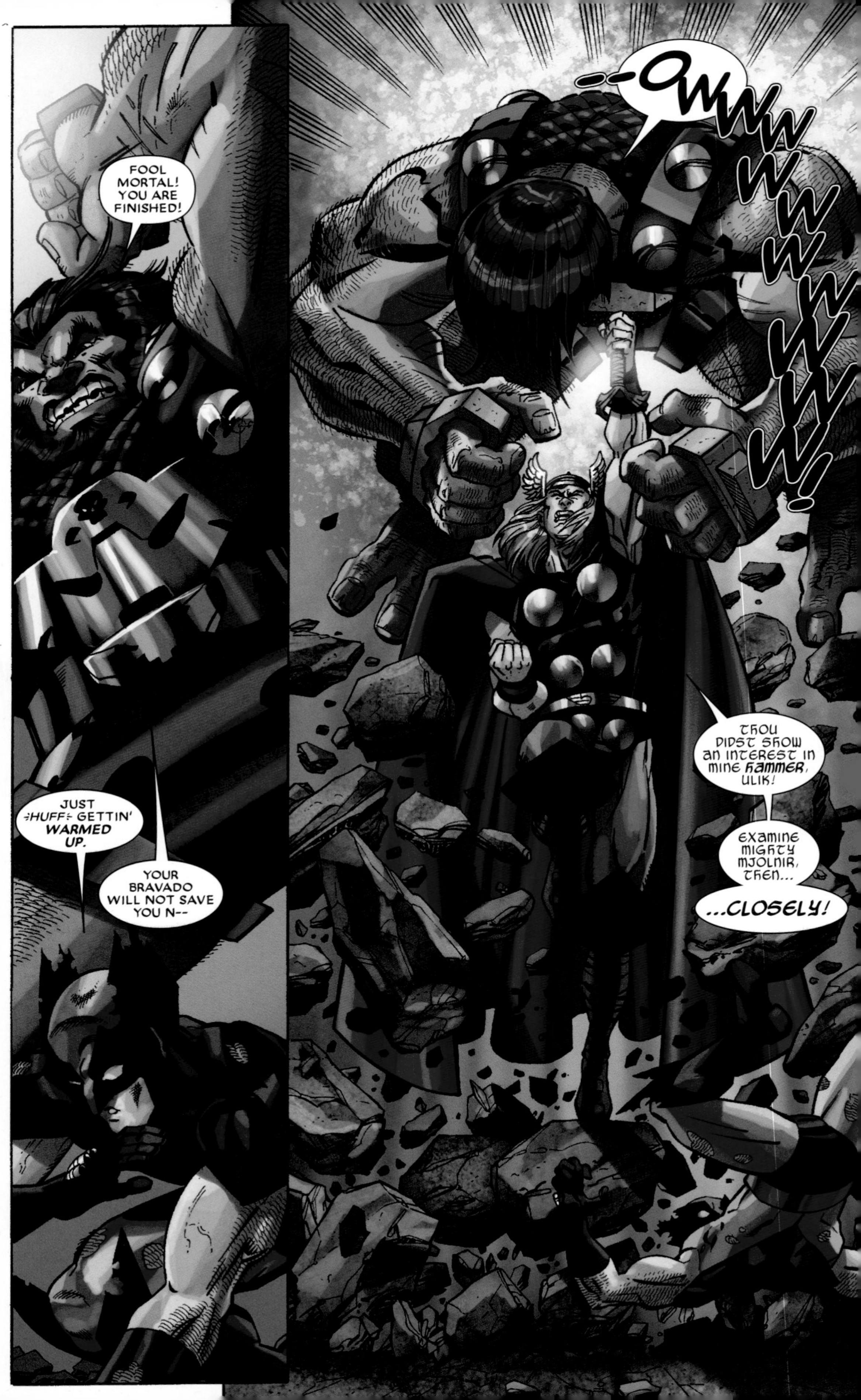
FOOL MORTAL! YOU ARE FINISHED!
JUST =HUFF= GETTIN' WARMED UP.
YOUR BRAVADO WILL NOT SAVE YOU N--
--OWWWWWWWWW!
THOU DIDST SHOW AN INTEREST IN MINE HAMMER, ULIK!
EXAMINE MIGHTY MJOLNIR, THEN...
...CLOSELY!

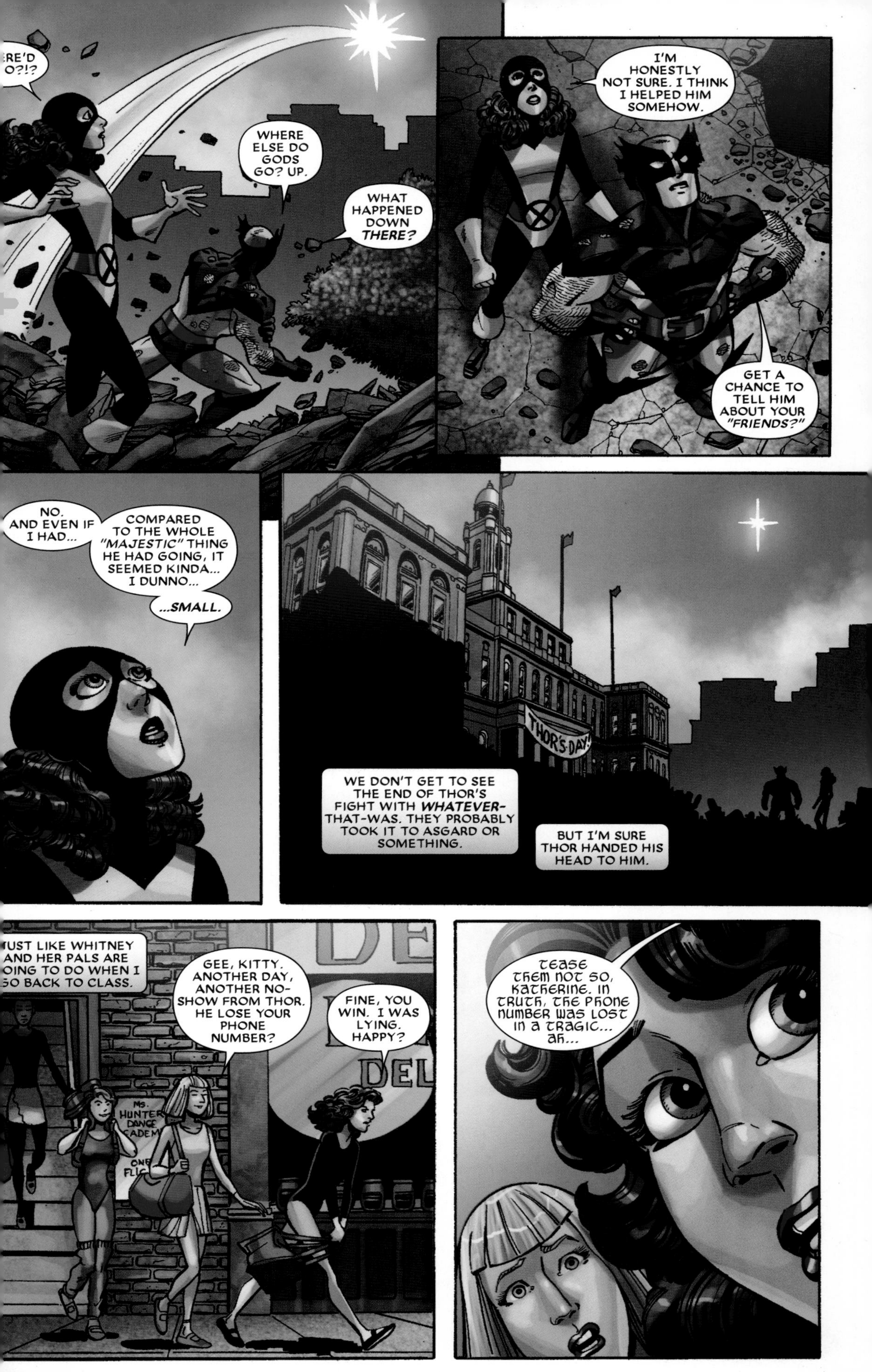

ERE'D
O?!?
WHERE ELSE DO GODS GO? UP.
WHAT HAPPENED DOWN THERE?
I'M HONESTLY NOT SURE. I THINK I HELPED HIM SOMEHOW.
GET A CHANCE TO TELL HIM ABOUT YOUR "FRIENDS?"
NO. AND EVEN IF I HAD...
COMPARED TO THE WHOLE "MAJESTIC" THING HE HAD GOING, IT SEEMED KINDA... I DUNNO...
...SMALL.
THOR'S DAY!
WE DON'T GET TO SEE THE END OF THOR'S FIGHT WITH WHATEVER-THAT-WAS. THEY PROBABLY TOOK IT TO ASGARD OR SOMETHING.
BUT I'M SURE THOR HANDED HIS HEAD TO HIM.
UST LIKE WHITNEY AND HER PALS ARE OING TO DO WHEN I O BACK TO CLASS.
GEE, KITTY. ANOTHER DAY, ANOTHER NO-SHOW FROM THOR. HE LOSE YOUR PHONE NUMBER?
FINE, YOU WIN. I WAS LYING. HAPPY?
TEASE THEM NOT SO, KATHERINE. IN TRUTH, THE PHONE NUMBER WAS LOST IN A TRAGIC... AH...

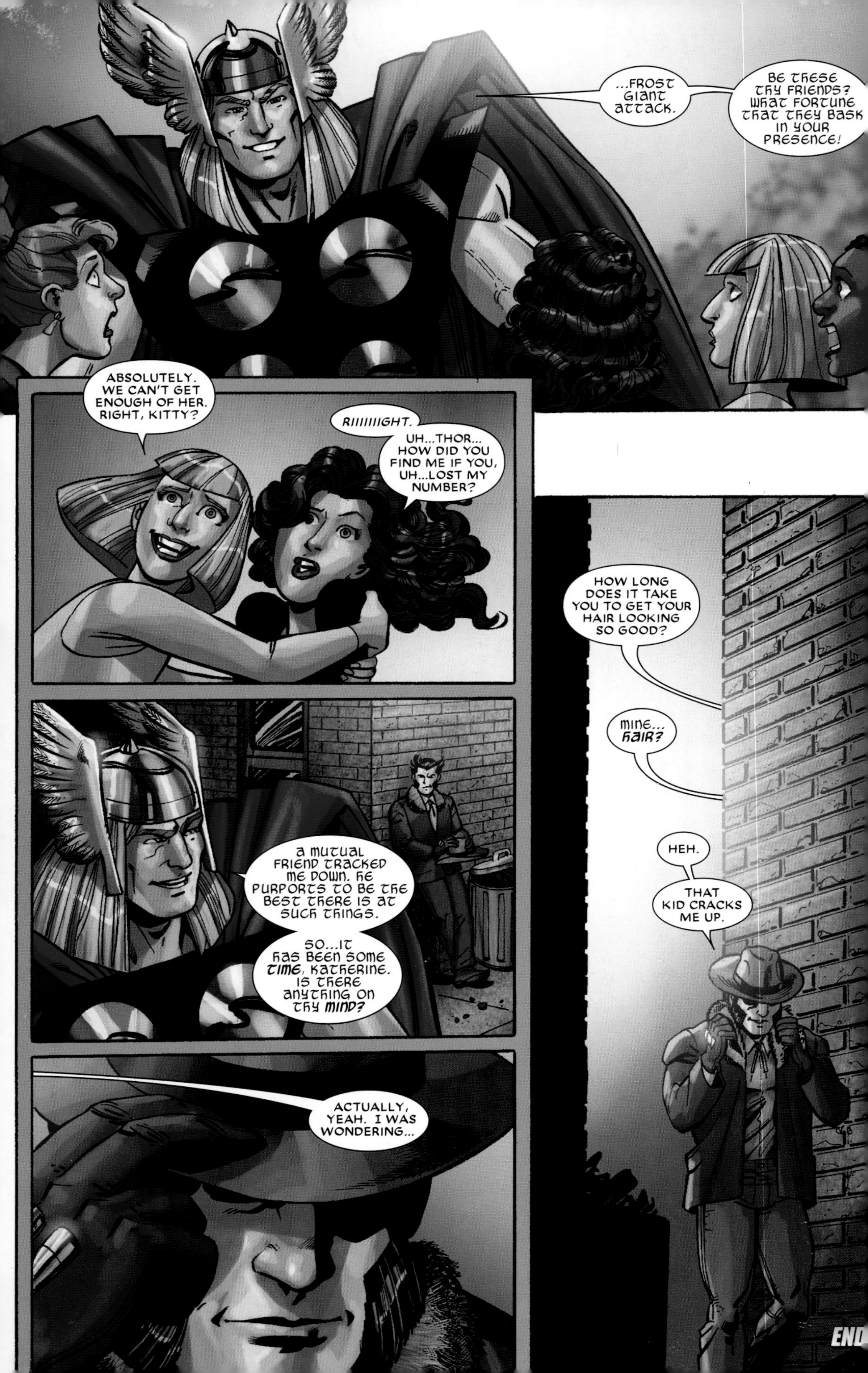
...FROST GIANT ATTACK.
BE THESE THY FRIENDS? WHAT FORTUNE THAT THEY BASK IN YOUR PRESENCE!
ABSOLUTELY. WE CAN'T GET ENOUGH OF HER. RIGHT, KITTY?
RIIIIIIIGHT.
UH...THOR... HOW DID YOU FIND ME IF YOU, UH...LOST MY NUMBER?
A MUTUAL FRIEND TRACKED ME DOWN. HE PURPORTS TO BE THE BEST THERE IS AT SUCH THINGS.
SO...IT HAS BEEN SOME TIME, KATHERINE. IS THERE ANYTHING ON THY MIND?
ACTUALLY, YEAH. I WAS WONDERING...
HOW LONG DOES IT TAKE YOU TO GET YOUR HAIR LOOKING SO GOOD?
MINE... HAIR?
HEH.
THAT KID CRACKS ME UP.
END